W9-BLK-770

Dragon Slayers' Academy™

HELP! IT'S
PARENTS DAY AT DSA

By Kate McMullan
Illustrated by Bill Basso

GROSSET & DUNLAP

Visit us at www.abdopublishing.com

Spotlight, a division of ABDO Publishing Company, is a distributor of high quality reinforced library bound editions for schools and libraries.

This library bound edition is published by arrangement with Penguin Young Readers Group, a member of Penguin Group (USA) Inc.

This one's for you, Peter Ricci—K. McM.

For all the Open School WEeks
I have known—B. B.

Library of Congress Cataloging-in-Publication Data

McMullan, Kate.
  Help! It's parents day at DSA / by Kate McMullan ; illustrated by Bill Basso.
    p. cm. – (Dragon Slayers' Academy)
  Help! It is parents day at DSA
  Summary: Wiglaf faces the double embarrassment of having his wacky parents visit Dragon Slayers' Academy on Parents Day and starring in the school play as the brave but small knight, Sir Tinybottom.
  ISBN-13: 978-1-59961-125-9 (reinforced library bound edition)
  ISBN-10: 1-59961-125-2 (reinforced library bound edition)
  [1. Schools—Fiction. 2. Knights and knighthood—Fiction. 3. Dragons—Fiction. 4. Theater—Fiction.] I. Basso, Bill, ill. II. Title. III. Title: Help! It is parents day at DSA. IV. Series: McMullan, Kate. Dragon Slayers' Academy.

  PZ7.M47879Hd 2006
  [Fic]—dc22
                                                                      2006013403

Chapter I

"The dungeon gives me the creeps." Wiglaf shivered as he, Angus, and Erica trudged through an underground passageway of Dragon Slayers' Academy.

"Oh, cheer up, Wiggie," Erica said to him. "Headmaster Mordred said when we get to the dungeon, we get a surprise."

"Right," said Angus. "But my Uncle Mordred's surprises are mostly bad surprises."

"Welcome!" Lady Lobelia said as the students filed into the dungeon. They found places to sit on the cold, stone floor. "Welcome to the Lobelia de Marvelous Playhouse!"

"Welcome to what?" Wiglaf whispered.

"I should say welcome to the *future* Lobelia de Marvelous Playhouse," Lobelia said. "For I have hired a crew of carpenters, otherwise known as the student teachers, to turn this dreary dungeon into a fabulous theater. A theater that my dear brother Mordred insists must be named after me!" She clasped her hands to her heart. "And now I can tell you boys the surprise Mordred has in store for you. His scout, Yorick, has delivered invitations to all your mums and dads to come to the first-ever Parents Day at DSA!"

Parents Day? thought Wiglaf. *That* was *a surprise.* He hadn't seen his parents since the day he and his pet pig Daisy had left the crowded family hovel in Pinwick and set off for DSA.

Lobelia smiled. "Here's one of the invitations. I'll pass it around."

Angus leaped up and grabbed the piece of

parchment from his Aunt Lobelia. Wiglaf and Erica read it over his shoulder.

COME YE! COME YE!
TO PARENTS DAY AT DSA!
St. Spiffin's Day Morning, nine o'clock
COME MEET OUR FINE FACULTY!
COME TOUR THE DSA CASTLE!
COME SLEEP THROUGH A CLASS WITH YOUR SON!
COME MAKE A BIG DONATION TO DSA!
P.S. DON'T FORGET YOUR MONEY BAG!

"I get it now," Angus whispered. "This is one of Uncle Mordred's money-making schemes!" He sighed. "I love my mother. But I'm not sure I want her showing up here."

Wiglaf nodded. He loved his parents, too. But they could be so embarrassing. His mother wore a bread basket on her head to protect her in case the sky should fall, which, she was sure, might happen any day. His father liked to show off the talent that had won him the Pinwick Belching Championship. What would the other boys think of his parents?

"This is bad," Erica said in a low voice. "I know Mumsy or Popsy will blurt something out, and that will be the end of my secret."

Wiglaf and Angus were the only DSA students who knew that Erica was a girl. And not just any old girl. A princess! She had disguised herself as a boy and had come to DSA because, more than anything, she wanted to be a great dragon slayer like her hero, Sir Lancelot. All the other boys at DSA thought she was a boy, too, and called her Eric.

Wiglaf passed the invitation to the boys in the row behind him. He raised his hand. "Lady Lobelia, when is St. Spiffin's Day?" he asked.

"Two weeks from today," said Lobelia. "Now, I'll tell you *my* surprise. I've written a wonderful play to be performed on Parents Day. A play with a part for every single DSA student! It tells the story of a brave knight."

"Oooh, make me the knight," Erica chanted softly. "Make me the knight!"

"My play opens with peasants singing—" Lobelia stopped. "Did I mention that my play is a musical? It is! The peasants sing a song about a wicked dragon who has captured a royal princess. It goes like this."

Lobelia sang:

> "With a hey nonny nonny,
> Diddle diddle, hi-dee-doo,
> We are superstitious peasants,
> But we know a thing or two!"

Superstitious peasants, Wiglaf thought. That's exactly what his parents were. Molwena was always tossing salt over her shoulder to ward off bad omens. Fergus was sure that bathing caused madness, so he'd never had a bath in his life. What if the other boys teased him because his dad smelled bad?

"There's a big fight scene at the end,"

Lobelia went on. "The knight slays the dragon and rescues the princess. Then the knight's loyal men and the princess's ladies-in-waiting dance the Garter Trot. And they all live happily ever after!"

"I just had an awful thought," whispered Erica. "What if Lobelia casts me as the princess? No way will I play a dopey princess."

"Brother Dave, the librarian, has been up late many a night copying scripts for each of you," Lobelia said. "When I call your name, and give you your part, come up and get your script. Start learning your lines tonight, boys. And your songs. Our first rehearsal will be right after lunch tomorrow. The following boys will play peasants:

"Chadbroth, Knockworm, Liverlot, Meechum, Blogwit, Pernroth..." read Lobelia. The list went on and on. Wiglaf expected to hear his name called at any minute. After all, he *was* a peasant.

"If I'm the knight, I could wear the new suit of armor I just ordered from the Sir Lancelot Catalog," Erica whispered.

"Bragwort," Lobelia kept reading, "Garbath, Nostrol, Fleabane, and Eric."

"That's so funny," Erica said. "For a second, I thought Lobelia called my name."

"I did call your name, Eric," said Lobelia. "Come pick up a script."

"You mean...I'm a...peasant?" Erica gasped. "That is so not right! I'm made for the part of the brave knight!"

"Sorry," said Lobelia. "Remember, there are no small parts, only small actors."

Erica took her script and returned to her spot on the floor. She sat down, boiling mad.

Lobelia looked down at her cast list.

"The dragon," Lobelia said, "will be played by Barley, Charlie, Farley, and Harley Marley."

"Awww right!" cried the four burly Marley brothers. "Dragon time!"

"You can share," Lobelia said, handing Harley a script. "You don't have many lines. Now, the knight's loyal men shall be played by Hockbit, Scrimbarth, Peawallow, Fopslippers, Stopgargle..." Wiglaf and Angus listened eagerly, but Lobelia did not call either boy's name.

"She's forgotten us!" Angus smiled. "Now we won't have to be in this stupid play!"

Wiglaf hoped it wasn't true. He had never been in a play. He wanted to be in this one, no matter how small his part.

"Now, for the royal princess." Lobelia smiled. "It's a big part, with lots of singing and dancing, and it shall be played by..."

All the boys held their breath in fear.

"...by my very own nephew, Angus!"

"What?" cried Angus. "It shall *not*!"

"Oh, yes, it shall," said Lobelia.

"No! I won't do it, Auntie Lobelia," cried Angus.

"This is a boys' school, Angus," said Lobelia. "Boys have to take girls' parts. And that's that."

"How about if I play a peasant?" Angus pleaded desperately. "I'd make a *great* peasant." He began to sing, "Honny nonny donny ponny!"

Lobelia ignored him.

"You're just doing this to get back at my mother!" Angus cried.

"Am not!" said Lobelia. "Why would I want to do that?"

"Because she's your big sister," said Angus. "And she used to boss you around when you were little."

"Still does," muttered Lobelia.

"Maybe so," said Angus. "But you don't have to take it out on me. It isn't fair!"

"Don't worry, Angus," whispered Wiglaf.

"We'll get you out of this, somehow."

"You boys will be ladies-in-waiting," Lobelia said. "Knickerknot, Percelipps..."

Wiglaf kept hoping to hear his name called, but he didn't. He wasn't expecting a big part. After all, he was the shortest boy in the whole school. And he wasn't much to look at. Yet he deserved a small part. Had Lady Lobelia completely forgotten about him?

"And finally," said Lobelia, "the part of the brave knight shall be played by—Wiglaf!"

Wiglaf's mouth dropped open. "Me? The brave knight?" All right! He jumped up to get his script. How proud his parents would be to see their son, the star of the play!

"Congratulations, Wiglaf!" said Lobelia as she handed him a script.

"Thank you." Wiglaf grinned.

Erica tried not to look jealous. "If I couldn't be the knight, I'm glad it's you, Wiggie."

"Lady Lobelia?" called Bragwort. "You never told us, what's your play called?"

"It's called *The Tale of Teeny Sir Tinybottom*," replied Lobelia. She turned and gave Wiglaf a wink. "You're such a teeny little lad. You're perfect for the part!"

Chapter 2

"Yoo-hoo, Tinybottom!" Harley Marley called to Wiglaf from across the DSA dining hall. All the boys cracked up, laughing.

"Very funny," muttered Wiglaf as he stood in the breakfast line with Erica and Angus.

"I can't believe I'm a peasant," said Erica.

"I can't believe I'm a princess," Angus said as he picked up a plate. "Wanna trade?"

"No, sorry," said Erica. "I'd rather be a peasant than a princess."

"I don't know which is worse," Angus grumbled, "the stupid play or my mom showing up at school. She'll start bossing everyone around. It'll be awful!"

"Bossy isn't so bad," said Erica, moving up in the line. "My Popsy is sweet, but he's not exactly the brightest torch in the banquet hall, if you know what I mean. And Mumsy is always chattering on. She never stops talking."

"My mother smells like the big batches of cabbage soup she makes each day," said Wiglaf. "And my father is always telling the worst jokes."

Wiglaf waited for Angus or Erica to tell him that wasn't so bad.

But Angus said, "Poor you. Cabbage really stinks!"

Erica said, "Bad jokes are awful."

Wiglaf swallowed. Were Fergus and Molwena going to be the most embarrassing parents at Parents Day?

They were now at the front of the breakfast line.

"What are these things?" Erica asked Frypot the cook as he plunked blackened blobs onto their plates. "They look worse than eels."

"Moat-scum muffins," said Frypot. "Best I could do, what with so few eels in my traps these days." The cook scratched his beard thoughtfully. "I wonder if poachers are sneaking into the moat and stealing my eels."

Wiglaf and Angus exchanged worried glances. Not long ago, they had rescued a baby dragon. A baby dragon who loved swimming in the castle moat and slurping up eels. A baby dragon who was supposed to stay up in the library with Brother Dave, but often didn't.

"They're burnt," said Angus as a pair of muffins clattered onto his plate.

"Only on the outside," said Frypot. "Next!"

"Let's go up to the library later," Wiglaf whispered to Angus as they made their way to the Class I table. "There's *something* we have to check out—and I don't mean a book."

"Brother Dave?" Wiglaf pushed open the library door. The monk had fallen asleep while lettering a play script. His head rested on his arms. Worm, the baby dragon, lay sleeping at his feet.

When he heard Wiglaf's voice, Worm slithered out from under the table and lunged at him, burbling, *"Mmmmmmommy!"*

Wiglaf stroked the shiny scales on his long, green neck. Wiglaf was the first one Worm had seen when he had hatched from his dragon egg, so he thought Wiglaf was his mom.

Worm bounded over to Angus. He sat on his hind legs and held out a paw for a treat.

"You have to earn your treats," said Angus. "Worm, stay!"

The dragon held still as a statue.

Angus waited. Then he said, "Release!"

Worm started running in circles.

"Worm," said Angus. "Flame up!"

Worm shot fire from his snout. WHOOSH!

"Good Worm!" Angus felt in his pocket for an eel treat. But all he found was part of a burnt muffin, which he'd pocketed. He held it out to Worm.

Worm snapped it up and quickly spat it out. BONK! It hit Brother Dave right in the bald spot.

"St. Marvin's mittens!" exclaimed Brother Dave, jumping up. "There art better ways to awaken a sleeping monk than with a stone!"

"Sorry, Brother Dave," said Angus. "It was an accident. And it was a muffin. Not a stone."

Worm hopped over to the librarian. He licked his head with his pink, forked tongue.

Then he bounced back to Wiglaf and flipped over onto his back. Wiglaf began rubbing his smooth, white belly. Worm's whole body rumbled with a happy purr.

"Brother Dave?" said Wiglaf as he rubbed. "We think Worm's been sneaking into the castle moat and eating all the eels."

"Hast thou, Worm?" exclaimed the monk.

The dragon just kept purring.

"He needs to stay here with you and only fly out at night," Wiglaf went on. "Or else Mordred will spot him."

"What if Worm shows up on Parents Day?" added Angus. "It'll be a disaster."

"Worrieth not, lads," said Brother Dave. "I shall keep mine eye upon this dragon."

"Thanks, Brother Dave," said Wiglaf. Then he and Angus headed off to rehearsal.

As they walked into the dungeon, Wiglaf saw that a wooden platform had been built at the far end of the room to serve as a stage.

"Heads up, actors!" Lobelia said. "Here's the most important thing—the show must go on. No matter if you flub your line or your wig falls off, the show must go on. Got that?"

All the students nodded.

"Good." Lobelia smiled. "Read-through, Act I, Scene I. Peasants, you're on!"

Erica led the peasants onto the stage.

"Peasants, you hum as Sir Tinybottom and his loyal men enter, stage left," called Lobelia.

Wiglaf and his loyal men climbed onto the stage. Lobelia handed out brooms. "These are your steeds," she said. "Mount up and ride!"

Wiglaf felt silly, straddling the broom and prancing around the stage on a pretend horsie.

"Gallop, Tinybottom!" called Lobelia. "Good! Peasants, begin your song."

The peasants began singing:

> *"With a hey nonny nonny,*
> *Diddle diddle, hi-dee-doo,*
> *We are superstitious peasants,*
> *But we know a thing or two!*
> *Dismount, good sirs, we beg you,*
> *Take a seat upon our wagon,*
> *While we sing for you the story*
> *Of the princess and the dragon!"*

"Sir Tinybottom? Loyal men? When you

hear the word 'dismount,' get off your steeds," called Lobelia. She ruffled through her script. "Now, where was I?"

"A peasant asks the knight who he is," said Erica. "And the knight sings his first song."

"Thank you, Eric." Lobelia gave a signal.

Wiglaf stood up. He began singing softly:

> *"Sir Tinybottom is my name,*
> *And as a knight, I gained my fame,*
> *By slaying dragons young and old,*
> *I'm teeny, yes, but also bold!"*

The loyal men sang out:

> *"He's teeny, yes, but also bold!"*

"Louder next time, Wiglaf," said Lobelia. "Very good, peasants. Keep singing."

Erica led the peasants in singing:

> *"With a hey nonny nonny,*

'Twas a princess so good-looking
A dragon flew her to his cave,
And said, 'Princess, start cookin'!'
The princess said, 'Oh, Dragon,
by the scales on your chin,
True princesses never cook,
we only order in.' "

"Yes! Now, Angus? On the word 'princess,' you enter and sing the princess lines. Marley brothers? On the word 'dragon,' come dancing in the way I showed you."

The peasants began singing again:

"With a hey nonny nonny,
'Twas a princess so good-looking . . ."

Angus trudged onto the stage.
"Yoo-hoo, prin-cess!" called some boys.
"Shut your traps!" yelled Angus.
"Shush!" called Lobelia.
Angus glared at his aunt.

Lobelia only turned to the peasants and shouted, "Sing!"

"A dragon flew her to his cave . . ."

The Marley brothers entered in a line. Each held the waist of the brother in front of him and kicked in all directions.

"Together now, dragon," directed Lobelia. "Kick right! Kick left!"

"Ow!" yelled Farley. "Barley kicked me!"

"Did not!" yelled Barley. "It was Harley!"

With that, the Marley brothers began pushing, shoving, and punching one another.

"Marley dragon!" yelled Lobelia. "Behave! Angus? Sing!"

Angus hardly opened his mouth as he sang,

"Dragon, by the whiskers on your chin . . ."

"Scales!" Erica stage-whispered.

"Thank you, Eric," said Lobelia. "Did you ever see a dragon with whiskers, Angus? No!"

"Make me a peasant!" begged Angus. "Please, please, please, Auntie!"

Lobelia folded her arms across her chest and said, "Not a chance."

Chapter 3

"**A**tten*tion!*" The headmaster swept into the DSA dining hall. His red velvet cloak rippled out behind him. He held a clipboard.

"Parents Day is only ten days away. Oh, it's going to be a big day!" Mordred grinned, his gold front tooth gleaming. "What with donations, contributions, and dunning parents who haven't paid tuition, my money bags will be overflowing!" His violet eyes spun joyously at the thought of so much gold.

Tuition! Wiglaf frowned. DSA tuition was seven pennies. He still owed all seven.

Mordred glanced at his clipboard. "Parents Day at DSA will begin with a welcome cheer by the winner of the Parents Day Cheer-Writing Contest."

"That'll be me!" said Erica. She took out a notebook and began scribbling.

"Other events," Mordred went on, "will include a stalking demonstration by Sir Mort's class, a stabbing demonstration by Coach Plungett's class, a weapons-wielding demonstration by Master X's class, and plenty of time at the brand-new Ye Olde DSA Gift Shoppe where you can purchase wonderful presents for your parents to take home."

As he listened, Wiglaf's thoughts turned to his parents. Yes, they were embarrassing. Still, he was looking forward to seeing them. He pictured his father's bloodshot eyes and yellow beard, always filled with supper crumbs. And his mother's chin mole.

"How's this for the cheer?" Erica said. She began whispering it to Wiglaf and Angus.

"Say ho! Say hey! Say hi to DSA!"

We'll show you what we've got!
You'll like it quite a lot!
Say ho, say hey, for good old DSA! Yay!"

"Not bad," said Angus.

"Back to your lunch, lads," Mordred checked his clipboard. "Except for Wiglaf."

Wiglaf froze as the headmaster strode over to the Class I table.

"You!" Mordred boomed. "Haven't paid a single penny of your tuition!"

"No, sir," said Wiglaf. "I haven't."

In truth, he washed dishes for Frypot most nights as payment to the school. But, somehow, Frypot never remembered to explain this arrangement to Mordred.

"Well, my boy," said Mordred. "If I don't have seven pennies from you by the end of Parents Day, I'm kicking you out of school."

"Uncle Mordred!" cried Angus. "No!"

"Mind your own beeswax, nephew!" said Mordred as he strode off.

Wiglaf swallowed hard. How would his parents ever come up with seven pennies by the end of Parents Day? Good-bye, DSA!

"Don't worry, Wiggie," said Erica. "We'll think of something. We've got time. There's no way we'd let you leave here."

The following week, Wiglaf didn't have a minute to spend worrying. Every day there was a play rehearsal. He worked hard to learn his lines and songs. Erica helped him. She had his part down cold. And everyone else's, too. Whenever somebody forgot a line, Erica piped up with the next few words until he got going.

In the afternoons after Stalking Class and Slaying Class, the boys scrubbed the classrooms, hallways, and dining hall. Mordred wanted the school spotless for Parents Day. Only at night, when he lay on his cot in the Class I dorm, did Wiglaf's thoughts turn to those seven pennies he didn't have.

"Don't worry, Wiggie," Erica kept saying. "We'll think of something."

But she said the same thing to Angus whenever he whined about his part in the play. And, so far, he was still standing on the stage every day at rehearsal and playing the part of the princess.

One night, just before torches out, Erica came over to Wiglaf and Angus's cots. "This is the best cheer I've written. Listen," she said.

"For DSA parents, we give a cheer!
Hooray! Hooray! You're finally here!
With our teachers, you will talk!
We will show you how we stalk!
We will show you how we slay
Practice dragons filled with hay.
We hope you'll see on Parents Day,
How much we love DSA! Yay!"

"You'll win the contest for sure," said Wiglaf. He tried to sound cheerful. Yet, inside, he felt anything but cheerful. He couldn't believe that soon he might be leaving DSA forever.

Every day, the dungeon looked less like a dungeon and more like the Lobelia de Marvelous Playhouse. A curtain hung in front of the stage. The scenery was painted—a peasant village and a dragon's cave.

"Dress rehearsal today!" Lobelia said one afternoon. "Go to the rack and find the costume with your name on it. Put it on and we'll begin!"

Wiglaf was excited. He had never worn armor before. He waited while everyone grabbed their costumes. Then he walked over to the rack, expecting to see a fine, silvery suit of armor. Instead, he saw a tiny suit of dull gray metal. It was so small! How could he ever fit into such a tiny, little costume? Surely, there had been some mistake.

Lobelia rushed over to him. "Let me help

you into your costume," she said. She plucked the breastplate off the rack and pulled the straps tightly around Wiglaf.

"Ouch!" he said.

"Suck in your gut, Wiglaf." Lobelia gave another tug. "There!" She buckled him in.

Wiglaf could hardly breathe.

"I know it's small," said Lobelia as she buckled on the leg protectors. "But you, Sir Tinybottom, need a tiny costume so you'll look as teeny as possible. Don't you agree?"

"Uhhhhh," Wiglaf wheezed.

"Good!" Lobelia set a tiny helmet on his head and rushed off to help one of the loyal men.

The helmet was so tight! And its white, feathered plume drooped down over his face.

"Oh, you are tough!" yelled Harley Marley.

"Hey, itty-bitty Tinybottom!" yelled Farley.

"Cut it out," Wiglaf told them. Then he caught sight of Angus. He was wearing a wig of blonde curls. It was topped by a crown. Lobelia was fastening the buttons of his floor-length, lavender gown.

"This is cruel, Auntie!" Angus wailed.

"Nonsense!" Lobelia fluffed a frill of lace at his collar. "You make such a pretty princess. Doesn't he, boys?"

Chapter 4

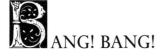ANG! BANG!

"Up and at 'em, lads!" Frypot stood at the doorway of the Class I dorm, banging on a skillet with his soup ladle. "Tomorrow is Parents Day at DSA. Who knows what that makes today?"

"St. Blithin's Day?" called out Torblad.

"No," said Frypot. "Bath day!"

The room grew still. Even Wiglaf, who'd once had a bath, couldn't believe his ears.

"Mordred's orders. Your parents don't want to find you stinking to high heaven," Frypot said. "So grab a towel and get out to the castle yard, on the double!" Off Frypot went to wake the Class II and Class III boys.

Torblad burst into tears. "Everyone knows that bathing causes madness!" he cried.

"That's only a superstition," Wiglaf said. "I had a bath once."

"See?" cried Torblad. "See? I'm not taking a bath and ending up like Wiglaf!"

"Oh, go blow your nose, Torblad," said Erica.

The Class I lads began rummaging under their cots for towels and clean underwear. Wiglaf and Angus found theirs and headed for the door.

"Erica?" whispered Wiglaf as they went. "What are you going to do?"

"Right," whispered Angus. "After all, you are...well, you know."

"I know," said Erica. "But I foresaw this problem. I have a note from home." She unfolded a sheet of parchment that said:

To: Headmaster, Dragon Slayers' Academy
Eric may participate in gym class and all

*sports, but he is not to take a bath. Ever. No
matter what.
Sincerely,
His parents,
Barbara and Kenneth
P.S. We mean it!*

"I wish I'd thought of that," said Angus as
they headed out into the yard.

"No bath, eh?" said Frypot, taking the
parchment note. "Then no bath it is."

Erica turned to Wiglaf and Angus. "I think
I'll go up to the library," she said. "And check
on *something*."

"Excellent," said Angus as she took off.

"Come, lads," said Frypot. He led Wiglaf
and Angus over to a huge kettle set over a
blazing fire. He gave the steaming water a stir
with a long stick. "Let's get started, shall we?"

"Egad!" cried Wiglaf when he saw the
bubbles. "Are we to bathe in boiling water?"

"Nah," said Frypot. "This is for your

uniforms. Strip 'em off, lads. Toss 'em in. Then go jump in the moat."

"The *moat?*" cried Angus. "It's freezing! And slimy. It smells worse than we do!"

"That it does," Frypot agreed. "But it's headmaster's orders. Go on now."

Wiglaf and Angus took off their uniforms and threw them into the bubbling cauldron. Then, wrapped in their thin towels, the boys scampered to the drawbridge. Dozens of unhappy lads were standing waist-deep in the murky moat, shivering.

"Let's jump in together," said Wiglaf. "On the count of three." They tossed their towels onto a branch of an overhanging tree. Wiglaf started counting. "One...two...two-and-a-half...three!" In they jumped.

Arrrg! It was freezing! Wiglaf began rubbing the worst of the dirt off an arm. He'd just started on his other arm when he felt something tickling his legs. Swamp grass, no doubt.

He reached down to brush it away. His hand hit something hard and...scaly.

"Angus...I feel...*something*," Wiglaf said.

"You d-d-d-do?" said Angus. His teeth chattered as he made his way over to Wiglaf. He reached under the water. His eyes widened. "I d-d-do, t-t-t-oo," he said.

A green head popped up out of the moat directly in front of them. The dragon got only as far as *"Momm—"* before Wiglaf lunged at him and shoved his head back under the water.

Seconds later, Worm's head bobbed up again, his yellow and red eyes sparkling.

Wiglaf knew that look. Worm wanted to play. The dragon scooted off and sucked in a mouthful of water. Then he leaped up, spraying Wiglaf and Angus.

"Cut it out, Worm!" Wiglaf whispered hoarsely. "The others will see you!"

Worm ducked down again.

Angus shielded his face with his arms as Worm bobbed up again, spraying.

"What's going on over there?" cried Torblad from the other side of the draw-bridge.

Wiglaf and Angus both pounced on Worm, and pushed his head back under the water.

"Nothing!" called Angus.

Wiglaf was horrified to see Torblad dog-paddling over to them.

Worm's head popped up again.

"Ahhhhhhhhhhhhhhhhhhhhhhhh!" screamed Torblad.

Wiglaf leaped at Worm and shoved him under again.

"What's wrong?" called Harley Marley from the far side of the bridge.

"Monster!" Torblad cried. "I saw a monster!"

"Nah!" Harley called back. "You're just going mad from having a bath."

Torblad shrieked and ran for the shore.

"Angus!" cried Wiglaf, splashing water every which way, trying to hide the dragon. "Your towel! Get it!"

Angus slogged through the marshy water and grabbed the towel from the branch. When he came back with it, Wiglaf threw it over Worm's head.

"Quick! Swim for the back of the castle!" Wiglaf said, still splashing. "Follow Mommy, Worm," he added. To his great relief, Worm swam after them.

"Look!" cried Torblad from the shore. "A swimming towel! Oh, blithers! I really have gone mad!"

Wiglaf, Angus, and Worm kept swimming until they reached the back side of the castle.

"Good, no one's around," Wiglaf panted, out of breath.

"Worm! Sit!" Angus commanded.

Instantly, Worm sat. Only his green head

stuck out of the murky water of the moat. His yellow and red eyes were fastened on Angus.

Angus stared back into Worm's eyeballs and said firmly, "I AM IN CHARGE. Tomorrow is Parents Day, Worm. And we need your help."

Worm didn't move a muscle.

Wiglaf caught sight of Erica running toward them on the bank.

"Worm's missing!" she cried. "He's not in the—" She stopped, staring at Worm's head poking out of the water. "—library."

Angus never looked away from Worm. "Tomorrow, Worm," he went on, "I shall bring you all your favorite treats for supper. Moat weed, moat slime, moat sludge, moat scum, and moat eels."

Strands of dragon drool began oozing from between Worm's lips.

"But only," Angus said sternly, "ONLY if you stay in the library all day. Got it, Worm?"

Worm blinked. A few more drips of drool hit the water.

"Now back to the library with you, on the double!" said Angus.

The dragon rose. He spread his wings, pushed off from the bottom of the moat, and started flapping.

Wiglaf felt a breeze as the dragon flew off toward the library tower.

"He understood, right?" Angus said. "I think he definitely got it."

"I hope so," said Wiglaf. But he wondered— could they trust a baby dragon?

Chapter 5

he big day dawned. Parents Day! Could this really be his last day at DSA? Wiglaf wondered as he struggled into his uniform. It was tight. Had it shrunk in the wash?

"I'm nervous," said Angus, trying to plaster down his hair. "My mom hasn't seen me in so long. I hope she won't think I've gotten plumper." He sucked in his gut.

"I'm nervous, too," said Wiglaf. "Nervous about my parents coming here. And nervous that I'll have to go home with them."

"I'll bet Mumsy blows my cover first thing," said Erica. "Then Mordred will know I'm a girl and give me the boot."

"Join the club." Wiglaf sighed. "My parents will never come up with seven pennies."

"Stop!" said Angus. "I won't be able to stand it if you two aren't here."

The three made their way to the castle yard. They saw a notice tacked to a tree and hurried over to read it.

PARENTS DAY AT DSA

WELCOME PARENTS CHEER

CAMPUS TOUR LED BY MORDRED DE MARVELOUS

GRAND OPENING OF YE OLDE DSA GIFT SHOPPE

(PARENTS MAY STAY AND SHOP OR

ATTEND CLASSES WITH SONS)

SCHOOL PICNIC LUNCH

DSA ALL-SCHOOL MUSICAL PRODUCTION

GOOD-BYES IN THE CASTLE YARD

As they studied the schedule, Mordred came rushing across the yard.

"Wiglaf!" he shouted as he passed, "remember—you owe me seven pennies! If I don't get them, you can start packing your bags."

Wiglaf's heart sank. "I might as well go up and start packing now," he muttered.

"Don't say that!" said Angus.

"We'll think of something," said Erica.

"I hope so." Wiglaf sighed. "Anyway, if this is my last day at DSA, I might as well enjoy it." He glanced up at the library tower. "Let's just hope Worm behaves himself."

"Atten*tion*!" Mordred called from the castle steps. He'd put on his best red velvet cape. Lobelia stood at his side in a gown of blue, with a matching pointed hat. The teachers—Sir Mort, Coach Plungett, Professor Pluck, and Master X—stood behind them.

"Today is the day we've all been waiting for," Mordred said. "And if I catch any of you sniveling little hooligans doing anything to—"

A blast of trumpets filled the air.

"Blazing King Ken's britches!" cried

Mordred as a pair of snowy steeds pulling a golden carriage galloped into the castle yard. "What's *that?*"

"Wouldn't you know it," said Erica. "My parents are first to arrive."

"That rig is solid gold!" Mordred's violet eyes nearly popped out of his head. "I wonder if it's Parents Day at Knights Noble Conservatory," he muttered. "And these parents have lost their way. They can't be coming *here!*"

Wiglaf and everyone in the castle yard hardly dared to breathe as the carriage stopped. A footman jumped down from his seat and opened the carriage door. Out stepped a woman with neatly curled brown hair topped by a big, gold crown.

The queen smiled and waved. "Hallo, subjects! Hallo! It's us, Queen Barb and King Ken. No need to kneel.... Now where is my little darling?" The queen looked around as she continued to wave. "Mumsy's here! Waiting for a hug and a kiss!"

An older man with white hair and a white beard stepped out of the carriage after her. He wore a fur-trimmed hat that sat at a cockeyed angle on his head.

"I say, small golf course," he said.

"It's a school, Kenny," said the queen. "We've come to visit Er—"

"Mumsy!" Erica cried out before her mom finished saying her name. "Popsy!" She ran toward them and hugged them.

Mordred flew down the castle steps to greet the queen and king. He held out the hem of his cloak and bent his knees in a curtsy. Then he bowed so low that his head nearly scraped the ground.

"Welcome! Welcome!" he cried. "So gold of you to come!"

"I say!" said King Ken.

"Sir," said Erica, "these are my parents."

"Oh, so gold to meet you!" babbled the DSA headmaster. "So very gold!"

Queen Barb hardly bothered to look at the groveling headmaster. "So this is your school, darling? Not quite as grand as I expected." She hugged Erica to her. "Oh, it's been so lonesome around the castle without our daughter."

Wiglaf winced. Erica was right. Her mom hadn't been here two minutes, and already she was spilling the beans.

"So, you also have a daughter," Mordred said. "Where does she go to school?"

"She goes to Princess Prep!" Erica put in quickly. "And she loves it there!" Then she yanked her startled mother's hand. "Come on, Mumsy. I'll show you Old Blodgett, the practice dragon." She dragged her off.

"I say!" said King Ken, trotting after them.

Other parents began arriving. Among them were a mom and dad wearing matching

"We're from Toenail!" T-shirts. Torblad ran to greet them. A stocky man and woman entered the castle yard and all four Marley brothers whooped and ran to them.

"Any sign of your parents?" Angus asked.

"Not yet," said Wiglaf. What if they hadn't gotten the invitation? What if they didn't know when St. Spiffin's Day was? He looked around. Where were they?

"My mom is usually the first to arrive," said Angus. "I wonder where she is."

"Maybe she's stuck in traffic," said Wiglaf. "You know how Huntsman's Path can get backed up if a herd of sheep is crossing."

"If she doesn't come, that's okay," said Angus glumly. "Then she won't have to see me playing the stupid princess in the play."

All at once, Wiglaf smelled a foul, yet familiar odor. Cabbage soup! And there, through the gate, came Molwena and Fergus. Molwena reached into her apron pocket for some salt and tossed it over one shoulder.

"Where's our boy, then?" Fergus said. Then he pounded his chest and gave out a deafening belch.

"Mother! Father! Here I am!" Wiglaf ran to his parents. Angus trailed after him.

"Ah, Wiglaf!" Molwena hugged him, then held him at arm's length, looking him up and down. "Scrawny as ever, I see." She pulled a flask from her apron and handed it to him. "My good cabbage soup will soon put some meat on your bones."

"This is my friend, Angus," Wiglaf told his parents. "He's going to stay with us until his mom comes."

"What a fine, well-fed lad you are!" Molwena exclaimed.

Angus smiled at the compliment.

"Come. I'll show you around school," Wiglaf said quickly, hoping to avoid Mordred.

But the headmaster had already spotted his family.

"Hold up!" Mordred called. "I want a word with you!"

"Uncle?" said Angus as the headmaster approached. "Why isn't my mom here?"

"Oops!" said Mordred. "I must have forgotten to invite her."

"You what?" cried Angus.

"Get over it, nephew," said Mordred. "Turnipia doesn't enjoy this sort of thing. Move aside! I must speak with these peasants. Wiglaf, introductions!"

"Mother, Father, may I present Mordred de Marvelous, our honorable headmaster," Wiglaf said, exactly as Mordred had ordered all the boys to do.

"Marvelous, eh?" Fergus gave his armpit a scratch. "Say, what's that spot on your tunic?"

"Father!" cried Wiglaf. "No!"

"What? A spot?" cried Mordred.

"Right there." Fergus poked Mordred's chest with his finger. "Looks like snot."

"Snot?" cried Mordred, horrified. He looked down to see the stain on his garment. As he did, Fergus brought his finger up and thumped Mordred's nose.

"Gotcha!" cried Fergus. "Hah! The old snot joke. Works every time."

Angus was snorting to keep from laughing. Wiglaf wanted to cry.

"So, you're a joker, are you, Fergus of Pinwick?" Mordred growled. He pulled out a handkerchief and wiped at his nose. His plum-colored eyes bulged with fury.

"That's me," said Fergus proudly.

"Well, I've got some news for you," Mordred said. "And it's no joke." His nose twitched. "What's that terrible odor?"

"That's my cabbage soup," said Molwena proudly. "Tastes better than it smells. Like to try some, Marvelous?"

"No!" said Mordred. "If I want awful food, there's more than enough right here at DSA. What I want to say is this—your son still owes me seven pennies tuition."

"Does he now?" Fergus picked at a scab on his ear.

"That's right," said Mordred. "And if I don't have seven pennies from you by the end of Parents Day, I'm tossing your son out of school!"

Chapter 6

"Greetings!" Mordred called to all the assembled parents and students from the castle steps.

"I can't believe Uncle Mordred didn't invite my mom on purpose," Angus muttered. "He and Auntie Lobelia can't stand her, but still. She is my mom."

Wiglaf threw an arm around his friend's shoulder. "At least now you don't have to worry about her seeing you play the princess."

"Quiet, please!" called Mordred. "One of our students has written a welcome cheer. Eric?"

Erica stepped forward holding two flags emblazoned with the DSA crest. *Why was she scowling?* Wiglaf wondered. She began cheering in a dull voice and waving the flags as if she barely had the strength to hold them.

> *"Welcome daddies, mommies, too!*
> *DSA is counting on you!*
> *Counting on you to do what you're told,*
> *Counting on you to give us your gold!*
> *Give us your loot and give us your stash,*
> *Give us your treasure chests full of cash!*
> *Give us your silver! Your pennies, too.*
> *(We don't take checks or IOUs.)*
> *So if your son likes DSA,*
> *It's time for you to pay, pay, pay!"*

The parents clapped politely.

"That wasn't her cheer," whispered Wiglaf.

"Let me take a wild guess who wrote it," said Angus. "Uncle Mordred."

Mordred clapped loudly for the cheer. "Now, I shall lead a tour of the school," he said. "Follow me!" The parents hurried after him into the castle. Wiglaf and his parents brought up the rear. Angus tagged along.

Mordred looked around as the parents gathered at the castle entrance. "Where is that lovely royal couple? King Ken? Queen Barb? Eric! Bring your parents up front."

"No special treatment for us," called Queen Barb. "We like to mix with our subjects now and then!" She began waving.

"Harumph!" said Mordred. "Well, this is my office." He extended a gold-ringed hand toward it. "It's where I make big decisions. Such as what new and exciting classes I can offer to make the boys happy here." Mordred beamed at the parents. "Next stop, the DSA Hall of Fame."

He led the way up the stairs.

"Here are the statues of Sir Herbert Dungeonstone and Sir Ichabod Popquiz." Mordred spoke in hushed tones. "Our noble founders."

Queen Barb bent forward and squinted.

"Take a look, Kenny," she said. "Don't they look like the thieves who stole all the funds from the Home for Aged Knights?"

"I say!" cried King Ken.

Mordred quickly slid between the statues and the king before he could get a good look.

"Falsely accused!" Mordred cried. "It wasn't all the funds, in any case. Only what they could carry. Anyway, it's just one of those colorful myths that are a part of the colorful history of our dear, old school."

Mordred sped up the tour, stopping only at various classrooms. In Stalking Class, Erica demonstrated a super Swamp Crawl for all the parents. In Slaying Class, Sir Mort had her perform a perfect Belly Buster. And in Weapons Class, she outdid every other student in Sword Play. At the end of her duel, everyone clapped. Everyone except Queen Barb, Wiglaf noticed.

"This way!" cried Mordred, leading the

tour down a hallway to the bottom of a staircase. "Now we'll go up to the lib— Confound it! What's that place called? That place with the things you lads read?"

"The library, sir," Erica answered. She looked worried.

Wiglaf's heart began to pound. Mordred had only been to the library once before. He didn't even know what it was! Wiglaf had thought it was the safest place in the whole school for Worm. But if Mordred led the tour there now, Worm would be discovered for sure.

Wiglaf shot Angus a frantic look.

Angus shrugged helplessly.

Mordred started up the stairs.

Suddenly, Fergus called, "Knock! Knock!"

Mordred turned slowly. He stared at Fergus, his purple eyes bulging.

"Uh...who's there?" said Mordred.

"Doughnut!" cried Fergus.

"Doughnut?" said Mordred. "Doughnut who?"

"Doughnut make me walk up all these steps!" cried Fergus.

The students and parents groaned.

Mordred's eyes glowed purple with fury.

But King Ken burst out laughing. "Jolly good joke! Must remember it, eh, Babs?"

"Heh, heh." Mordred laughed weakly, too. "Well, perhaps there *are* too many steps. I don't want to tire out our royal visitors." His eyes lit up. "I've got it. I'll take you straight to the gift shop."

As they set off, Wiglaf looked at Fergus with new eyes. His father had kept everyone away from the library! Even if Wiglaf had to leave school, Worm was safe. At least for now.

At the rear of the castle, the tour stopped at a wide doorway. Over it hung a brightly painted sign for Ye Olde DSA Gift Shoppe.

"Browse!" said Mordred, waving the parents inside. "Shop! Enjoy! You, too, pupils! Tell your parents what items you want. I'm sure they'll be glad to buy them for you!"

Erica was the first to drag her parents into the shop. Wiglaf, his parents, and Angus followed along.

"A DSA eel juice mug!" Erica cried. "Can I have it, Mumsy?" She started scooping up DSA pennants and DSA notepads. "Here's a DSA quill pen. You'd like that, Mumsy. And here's a DSA mead flask for you, Popsy!"

"Jolly good!" exclaimed King Ken.

"Darling, put those things back on the shelves," said Queen Barb quietly.

"What?" said Erica. "Why?"

Queen Barb sighed. "Aren't you ready to give up this silly notion of becoming a dragon slayer, darling?"

"Never!" said Erica. "I love it here. I've been Future Dragon Slayer of the Month more times than anyone. Right, Wiglaf? Right, Angus?"

Both boys nodded.

"We have some news for you, darling," said Queen Barb. "Isn't that right, Kenny?"

"Fill 'er up," replied King Ken, holding out the DSA mead flask.

"Come," said the queen. "Let's get a little fresh air and have a talk." With a wave to her subjects, she led the way out of the shop.

As she passed by, Erica cast a stricken look at Wiglaf and Angus. "I don't like the sound of this," she muttered.

"We'll come find you as soon as we can," Wiglaf promised.

The gift shop was mobbed. Wiglaf could hardly breathe as he stood surrounded by parents grabbing things from shelves stacked with DSA T-tunics, DSA sweat-leggings, and DSA jousting caps in S, M, L, and XL. There were framed portraits of the DSA headmaster, also available in S, M, L, and XL. There were DSA ale jugs. DSA ice chest magnets. Toy DSA thumbscrews and DSA scented candles. *What in the world would DSA candles smell like?* Wiglaf wondered. *Mildew? Mouse droppings? Old socks?*

At last, they managed to push their way out of the gift shop. Off they went to lunch in the castle yard.

"Eat with us," Wiglaf told Angus as they headed toward the big, colorful picnic cloths spread out on the grass.

"I'm not hungry," said Angus. "My mom's not coming. I'm about to make a total fool of myself in the play. This is the worst day of my life."

Angus not hungry? He really must be miserable, thought Wiglaf. "This isn't exactly the best day for me, either," he answered.

Erica and her parents were already sitting on a royal blue picnic cloth. As he drew near,

Wiglaf saw that Erica's eyes were red and puffy. Had she been crying? Erica never cried.

Erica jumped up as soon as she saw Wiglaf and Angus. "I have to talk to you," she said. "This is the worst day of my life!"

The three hurried over to the castle wall.

Erica wiped her eyes. "I have to leave DSA," she said in a shaky voice. "My parents are making me transfer to Princess Prep!"

Chapter 7

"Y ou're both leaving school?" wailed Angus. "I'll be left here all by myself!"

"Trust me," said Erica. "I don't want to go."

"Neither do I," said Wiglaf. "I like it here."

"Mumsy said she only let me come to DSA to get dragon slaying out of my system," said Erica, sniffing. "She says I can't be a knight because I'm a princess. I don't want to be a princess!"

"I know exactly how you feel," muttered Angus.

"Mumsy says it's time I started behaving like a princess," Erica went on. "At Princess Prep, I'll have to take classes like the Haughty

Look, the Princess Walk, and How to Order Subjects Around. Yuck!"

"Cheer up," said Wiglaf. "At least you won't live in the hovel with twelve brothers who are always beating you up."

"That sounds almost as bad as Princess Prep," Erica admitted. "Oh, we have to think of some way to stay here!"

When they returned to the picnic area, Wiglaf was startled to see Queen Barb tasting a spoonful of Molwena's cabbage soup.

"Interesting," said Queen Barb after she'd managed to swallow. "Kenny, dear, would you like to try some?"

"I say, Babs," said King Ken. "I'm smack in the middle of learning that joke."

"And the chump says back to you, 'Doughnut who?' Got that?" said Fergus.

Wiglaf thought his parents seemed very comfortable, lunching with royalty!

During dessert, Mordred appeared again

to deliver his lunchtime lecture on the Spirit of Giving at DSA. He cleared his throat. "Would you like your son to get all A's in school? No problem. Would you like to have the DSA dining hall named in your honor? It could happen. Or how about a turret sporting a big, brass plaque with your crest on it? Easy as pie. All you have to do is—"

"Knock! Knock!" Fergus called out.

"What? You again! Oh, all right...Who's there?" said Mordred grudgingly.

"Juan!" called Fergus.

"Juan who?" said Mordred.

And Fergus cried out, "Juan are our sons going to bring home some gold?"

"Yes! When?" cried the other parents. "That's what your ads promised!"

"Our boys were going to slay dragons and bring home their golden hoards!" called a mom.

Parents began chanting, "We want our

gold! We want our gold!"

Mordred's face grew brick red. "Be patient!" he cried. "Your sons are just starting to learn the ways of dragon slaying. It takes time! Now, as I was saying, you can have your crest engraved on a brass plaque in the entryway. All you—"

"Knock! Knock!" cried Fergus again.

Mordred's violet eyes bulged dangerously. "Who's there?"

"Kent!" cried Fergus.

"Kent who?" said Mordred.

"Kent you tell us when we'll get the gold?" cried Fergus.

"Yes! Yes!" cried the other parents. "We want our gold! We want our gold!"

Mordred's face was now a raging purple. "You have some nerve. You owe *me* seven pennies," he shrieked at Fergus. "Where's Master X? I want this lout out of here!"

But just then King Ken piped up. "Jolly,

jolly good jokes!" he cried. "I say! The school should have a joke-telling class!"

Fergus smiled. "Want to hear more? I can keep 'em coming."

"I say!" King Ken grinned.

"Knock! Knock!" called Fergus.

This time King Ken answered: "Hallo!"

"No, no," said Fergus. "You say, 'Who's there?'"

"Ah! I see!" said King Ken.

"Knock! Knock!" said Fergus.

"Back again, are you?" said King Ken.

"Blazing King Ken's britches!" Fergus shouted. "You've got it all wrong!"

The castle yard grew still. Wiglaf nearly choked on his dessert of jellied moat weed pie. His father had insulted the king! Would he be thrown in jail? Would he be put in leg irons?

King Ken slowly rose to his feet. "I say!" he said. "That's just what Babs said the time my royal pants caught fire."

"Tell us about it, sir!" said Molwena.

"Yes, yes!" cried the other parents.

"Oh, all right, go on," said Mordred irritably. He sat down on the castle steps.

King Ken smiled. "Jolly good, what?"

Queen Barb rose to her feet. "Let me tell our loyal subjects about it, Kenny," she said. She gave them a wave. "One freezing cold winter's day, Kenny went out for a stroll and froze his backside. He had no feeling in it at all. Numb as a log, he said."

"Mumsy!" Erica groaned.

"When he came home," Queen Barb said, "Kenny tried to thaw himself out by backing up to the roaring fire in the fireplace. His bum was still frozen solid, you see."

"Mumsy! Stop, *please!*" begged Erica.

"I happened to come in," Queen Barb went on, "and a good thing, too. Poor Kenny was way too close to the fire. His britches were all aflame. And I cried out—"

"Blazing King Ken's britches!" everyone in the yard called out.

Queen Barb smiled. "Exactly," she said. "The servants came and doused Kenny's backside with buckets of water. They saved him. But they couldn't save his britches. We had what's left of them mounted on red velvet. They're on view for all to see at the palace. You're all welcome anytime." The queen waved and sat back down.

Wiglaf glanced at Erica. She had her head in her hands. It seemed that even royal parents could be embarrassing.

Mordred stood up. "Well, I certainly enjoyed hearing that bit of royal lore, as I'm sure you did," he said. "All right, students. Lady Lobelia tells me it's time for you to report to the Lobelia de Marvelous Playhouse to get ready for the play. Parents, stay right where you are."

"You'll like the play," Wiglaf told his

parents as he got up. "I have a big part."

"Here's for luck!" said Molwena, tossing a whole handful of salt over Wiglaf's shoulder.

Wiglaf and his friends headed for the theater. As he went, Wiglaf heard Mordred saying, "My dear, dear DSA parents! Would you like your son to get all A's in school? No problem. Would you like to have the DSA dining hall named in your honor? It could happen..."

Chapter 8

ackstage, Wiglaf sat down. He shoved the little helmet on his head. "I wish I wasn't leaving...I'll miss you, Angus."

"That goes double for me." Angus stepped into his lavender gown. "Button me up, will you?"

Wiglaf had just started on the buttons when Erica ran in. She was carrying a big box.

"Here, Wiggie," she said. "It's my new suit of armor. I won't need it where I'm going. You can wear it in the play."

Wiglaf smiled. "Thanks, Erica!" He began putting on the silvery armor.

Erica pulled her peasant tunic on over her head. "I can't believe I'm leaving! My snotty cousin Bratilda goes to Princess Prep. I'll hate it there!"

Wiglaf put on the new Lancelot helmet. It was shiny silver. Its plume stood up straight. He tried out the visor, opening and closing it over his face.

"You look like a proper knight now, Wiglaf," said Angus.

Wiglaf watched as his friend put on his blonde, curly wig and set the crown on top of it. Poor Angus. He looked like he was going to be sick.

"Oh, Angus!" said Lady Lobelia, rushing over to him. "You make a perfectly lovely princess!"

"I don't think so!" boomed a loud voice.

Wiglaf turned to see a frowning woman in a large, lavender gown very much like the one Angus was wearing. She had long, blonde curls, too.

"Mom!" exclaimed Angus. "You're here!"

"And in the nick of time, from the looks of things," said Turnipia. "You're not going on stage in that costume."

"Uncle Mordred said he didn't invite you," Angus told her.

"He didn't," said Turnipia. "I heard about it from a peasant on Huntsman's Path this morning. Of course, I came right over." She eyed her son. "Now, lose the costume, mister."

Angus grinned. "I am so happy you came, Mom."

"I suppose this is your idea of a little joke, Lobelia," Turnipia said, glaring at her sister. "Were you trying to make fun of me?"

"Of course not, Turnipia!" cried Lobelia. "Angus is one of the leads. He plays the princess!"

"Not going to happen," said Turnipia.

Erica sprang up and unbuttoned Angus's buttons. He slipped out of the gown.

"Turnipia, you'll ruin my play...you always ruin everything for me," Lobelia sobbed. "There's no time for anyone else to learn the part! The parents are here! The show must go on!"

"Come, Angus," said Turnipia. "Let's go find some seats. This ought to be good." She grabbed Angus's hand and whisked him off.

"The show must go on," Lady Lobelia said. "But how? How?"

Wiglaf nudged Erica. "You could do it," he said. "You know everybody's part." And suddenly an idea popped into Wiglaf's head. "Erica! What if you show your parents what a natural you are at being a princess? Who knows? Maybe they'll decide you don't have to go to Princess Prep, after all."

A smile crept onto Erica's face. "It could work," she said. She jumped up and ran to

Lobelia. "I'll be the princess," she offered. She tore off her peasant garb and began putting on the lavender gown.

Wiglaf was happy to see Erica looking so hopeful. And Angus didn't have to be the princess. Now, if only he could think of a way for Mordred to let *him* stay at DSA, everything would be great.

On the other side of the curtain, Wiglaf could hear the parents taking their seats. All at once, it hit him. Wiglaf was going to be out onstage in front of hundreds of people! His heart began to thump as Lobelia stepped out in front of the curtain to greet the audience.

"It is my great pleasure to present my play, *The Tale of Teeny Sir Tinybottom,* written and directed by yours truly!"

The curtain went up and Sir Tinybottom rode his broomstick horse out onto the stage. Right behind him came his loyal men, galloping on their broomstick horses. The peasants began to sing:

"With a hey nonny nonny,
Diddle diddle, hi-dee-doo..."

It wasn't long before Sir Tinybottom and his loyal men were standing outside the cave where the dragon was holding the princess prisoner. Wiglaf began to sing:

"Sir Tinybottom is my name,
And dragon slaying is my game,
Come out now, dragon, from your cave.
I'm teeny, yes, but very brave!"

"That's me boy!" Fergus called out proudly for all to hear. Wiglaf turned red, but part of him felt happy as well.

The knight's loyal men sang the refrain, *"He's teeny, yes, but very brave!"*

This was the cue for the four Marley brothers in their bright green dragon costume to appear. But...where were they?

Wiglaf cleared his throat and sang the last two lines of his song, louder this time.

> *"Come out now, dragon, from your cave.*
> *I'm teeny, yes, but very brave!"*

Still no dragon.

Then Wiglaf heard shuffling feet behind him. Whew! The Marley brothers were coming, at last.

Wiglaf drew his sword.

There was a sudden yelp from the crowd.

Someone gasped. "Is that thing *real?*"

That's when the visor of Wiglaf's helmet clanked down over his face. He heard boys shouting, "Help! Run!" It sounded like his loyal men. Were they running offstage? This wasn't in the script. What was going on?

Wiglaf pushed up his visor and turned around. His eyes grew wide. He saw a green head attached to a long neck and a green, scaly

body. He saw a pink, forked tongue. And sharp, white fangs. He saw yellow eyes with cherry red centers. This was no dragon costume.

"Blazing King Ken's britches!" cried Wiglaf.

It was Worm!

Chapter 9

orm bounded across the stage toward Wiglaf. He wanted to play!

Wiglaf froze. What was he to do? Lobelia always said, "The show must go on!" It was up to him now.

Wiglaf rode toward Worm on his broomstick horse. As he drew closer, he waved his sword. "Have no fear, Sir Tinybottom's here!"

The audience cheered loudly.

"Bravo, brave knight!" yelled Turnipia. "Bravo!"

"It's only me, Worm," Wiglaf said under his breath. "It's Mommy."

Then Wiglaf began singing his dragon-fighting song:

"With a hey nonny nonny,
Nonny nonny hey, hey, hey,
Just you try to get Sir Tiny-B,
Come on, dragon, make my day!"

While the audience cheered again, Wiglaf whispered loudly to Worm, "Flame up!"

Twin flames shot from Worm's snout.

WHOOSH!

Wiglaf kept Worm riled up and flaming while he finished his song. He waved his sword. He galloped around the stage on his fake steed. When it was time to "slay" this dragon, Wiglaf knew just what to do. In a soft voice, he said, "Tummy rub, Wormie?"

Worm hit the floor and rolled over onto his back. Wiglaf raised his sword and pretended to do the dragon in. Then he fell to his knees, as if examining his kill, and began rubbing Worm's soft, white belly.

"*Mmmmm,*" Worm murmured happily.

Still on his knees, Wiglaf began singing to the princess:

> "Sir Tinybottom is my name,
> The wicked dragon I have slain,
> Come out now, princess, have no fright,
> I'm teeny, yes, but what a knight!"

From backstage, the loyal men sang,

> "He's teeny, yes, but what a knight."

The princess swept in from stage left, wearing a lavender gown. She walked with her head held high. She stopped and fixed Wiglaf with a haughty look. Over Worm's gentle purring, she sang:

> "Princess Belinda is my name,
> This dragon never more will flame,
> Now I am free, you are so kind,
> You're teeny, yes, but I don't mind!"

Her ladies-in-waiting appeared, and sang:

"He's teeny, but she doesn't mind!"

This was the cue for Sir Tinybottom to take the princess's hand and dance with her.

"Stay!" Wiglaf whispered to Worm.

The dragon stayed on his back, frozen to the spot.

Wiglaf rose to his feet. He took Erica's hand and the two of them began to dance. Wiglaf always dreaded this moment of the play, for Angus could not do the Garter Trot without stomping on Wiglaf's toes. But Erica tripped lightly over the stage, never once treading on his feet.

Now the loyal men ran back onto the stage. The princess ordered her ladies-in-waiting to dance with them. They all joined hands and danced the Garter Trot around Worm, who never moved a muscle.

The dance ended. The actors turned to face the audience. Together, they sang:

"With a hey nonny nonny
And a hey, hey, hey!
We hope we've entertained you
With our play, play, play!"

Everyone in the audience leaped up, clapping and cheering as the curtain came down.

"That's me boy, Wiglaf!" Molwena shouted.

"Remember that name!" Turnipia yelled. "He'll be famous one day!"

While the peasants took their bows, Wiglaf ran to Worm. "Release! Go home! Now!"

Worm rolled over and jumped up. He licked Wiglaf's face. Wiglaf shoved the dragon toward the back door of the ex-dungeon. "Go to Brother Dave! Shoo! I'll come see you later!"

Wiglaf zoomed back to the stage in time for his curtain call. He took Erica's hand and, while she curtsied to the audience, Wiglaf bowed. He really did feel like a star. So what if he was teeny Sir Tinybottom? The audience loved him.

After six curtain calls, the cast presented Lobelia with a big bouquet of roses. At last, the audience stopped clapping.

"Excellent, lads!" Mordred cried as he rushed backstage. "Ha! This will get your parents digging deep into their pockets for dear old DSA." He was beaming. "No rush to get out of your costumes. I've sent your parents back to Ye Olde DSA Gift Shoppe. Last chance to shop before good-byes in the castle yard...and safe trip home, Wiglaf," Mordred added with a wicked smile. Then he sped off.

Lobelia had arranged a tray of cookies backstage for a little cast party. Wiglaf snatched a few.

"I can't eat. But Worm deserves a real treat," he glumly told Erica. "And it may be the last time I see him."

"I want to say bye to Worm, too," said Erica. "Let's go now, Wiggie."

But before Wiglaf and Erica could change out of their costumes, Angus and Turnipia came backstage.

"Oh, well done, Sir Tinybottom," Turnipia said. "Star quality!" She turned to Erica. "And you were the perfect princess."

Erica smiled. "I hope my parents think so, too."

"When Worm—er, I mean—when the dragon showed up, you were great," Angus told Wiglaf. "And guess what?" He held up a large burlap bag. "Mom brought a goodie bag. We can really pig out in the dorm tonight."

Wiglaf's smiled faded. "I—I won't be in the dorm tonight, remember?"

"Why not?" asked Turnipia.

"I never paid my tuition," Wiglaf mumbled. "Headmaster Mordred won't let me stay."

"That's the silliest thing I've ever heard,"

said Turnipia. "That dreadful little brother of mine can be a real pain."

Wiglaf caught sight of Fergus and Molwena now.

"Good job, son!" Fergus began pounding him on the back.

"How'd you work that fake dragon?" Molwena wanted to know.

"It's, uh, hard to explain," said Wiglaf.

"Darling!" cried Queen Barb as she and the king hurried over to Erica. "What a performance!"

"You liked it?" asked Erica.

"I say!" said King Ken.

"This is me boy," Fergus told the king, still pounding Wiglaf on the back.

"I say!" said King Ken.

"Mumsy?" said Erica. "Did I do the Haughty Look all right?"

"To perfection!" said the queen.

"How was my Princess Walk?" asked Erica.

"Divine," said the queen.

"Did you like the way I ordered around my ladies-in-waiting?" asked Erica.

"Couldn't have ordered them better myself," said the queen.

"I am a born princess, Mumsy," said Erica. "You saw me with your own eyes."

"Yes..." said the queen.

"So why do I need to transfer to Princess Prep?" Erica said.

"Perhaps you have a point," said Queen Barb. She turned to the king. "What do you say, Kenny? Shall we let her stay here at DSA?"

"I say—yes!" said King Ken.

Erica's face lit up. Wiglaf thought he'd never seen her look so happy.

Parents Day worked out just fine for Erica, Wiglaf thought as he took off his silvery helmet. *And for Angus, too. Well, two out of three wasn't bad.*

Chapter 10

veryone made their way back to the castle yard. Many parents were loaded down with Ye Olde DSA Gift Shoppe bags. Wiglaf walked over to the gatehouse where Lobelia and Mordred were bidding farewell to the parents. Mordred held open a money bag for anyone who felt like tossing in some spare change.

"I've come to say good-bye, Lady Lobelia," said Wiglaf. "Good-bye, Headmaster Mordred. I've learned a good deal at DSA."

"Of course you have, boy," said Mordred. "Maybe if you scrimp on food, clothing, medicine, that sort of thing, you can save up seven pennies and come back."

"I'd like that, sir," said Wiglaf.

"Mordred!" a voice boomed. This time Wiglaf didn't have to turn around to know it was Turnipia. "A word with you, little brother!"

"Turnipia!" Mordred yelped. "How did you know about—I mean, so glad you got your invitation."

"You know perfectly well you didn't send me any invitation, Mordie," Turnipia growled. "Now what's this nonsense about Wiglaf leaving?"

"But he hasn't paid me," said Mordred in a whiny voice.

"I hereby establish the Turnipia de Marvelous Scholarship Fund for Promising Young Actors." Turnipia reached into her purse and pulled out a fistful of coins.

Wiglaf's heart beat with joy as Turnipia

counted, "One, two, three, four, five, six, seven," and dropped the coins into Mordred's money bag.

"There, Mordie," she said. "He's paid in full. And he's staying."

"Thank you!" cried Wiglaf. "Thank you!" Three cheers for bossy older sisters!

"Yes, Turnipia," said Mordred meekly.

Turnipia turned to Wiglaf. "Make sure he gives you a receipt," she said.

"Yes, ma'am," said Wiglaf. He spun around and took off for Fergus and Molwena.

"Mother! Father!" he cried. "Guess what?"

When they heard the news, Fergus began pounding Wiglaf on the back again. "Way to go, my boy. Stay here until Marvelous sends you home with some gold, eh?"

"You made a fine knight, Wiglaf," said Molwena. She hugged him to her. "Farewell, me boy. Don't let any cats cross your path, now. And run for cover if the sky starts falling.

Promise? And have a spoonful of soup before we go."

So Wiglaf did. He was so happy, it almost tasted good.

Molwena smiled and turned to Fergus. "Let us be off, Fergie. Or we won't have time to stop by Needleknock Village to see the colt born with two rear ends."

"Let us be off!" cried Fergus. Then he belched so loudly that Wiglaf felt the ground tumble.

As Fergus and Molwena headed for the castle gate, Harley Marley ran up to Wiglaf.

"Your dad is the best!" he said. "Can you belch like him?"

"No," said Wiglaf.

"Too bad," said Harley.

Turnipia bid all Angus's friends good-bye. Then she turned to her son.

"Good-bye, Angus," she said. "You boys

enjoy that goodie bag. And there's more where that came from."

"Thanks, Mom," said Angus. "Thanks for everything."

As Turnipia rode off, a team of snowy horses galloped into the yard, pulling the golden carriage. It stopped beside Queen Barb and King Ken, and the royals got in.

As the carriage circled the yard, Queen Barb poked her head out the window. "Farewell, subjects!" she called with a wave. "And good-bye, *Eric*!"

Erica grinned. "Bye, Mumsy! Bye, Popsy!"

King Ken stuck his head out the window, too, and called, "Knock! Knock!"

Everyone in the castle yard called back, "Who's there?"

King Ken grinned. "No idea, really. Bye-bye!"

"Good-bye! Good-bye!" cried all the DSA students, waving after them.

Wiglaf looked around. He saw DSA students, DSA teachers, and DSA student teachers. But no DSA parents.

"We survived Parents Day!" said Angus.

"All of our problems are over!" cried Erica.

As Wiglaf opened his mouth to add a cheer, he happened to glance up at the top of the castle. There, perched on the library tower like a bright green parakeet, sat Worm.

"Almost all of them, anyway," said Wiglaf.

The Campus of Dragon Slayers' Academy

∼ Our Founders ∼

Sir Herbert Dungeonstone

Sir Ichabod Popquiz

Sir Herbert and Sir Ichabod founded
DSA on a simple principle still held dear:
Any lad—no matter how weak, yellow-
bellied, lazy, pigeon-toed, smelly, or
unwilling—can be transformed into a fear-
less dragon slayer. After four years at
DSA, lads will finally be of some worth to
their parents, as well as a source of great
wealth to this distinguished academy.* ** ***

* Please note that Dragon Slayers' Academy is a strictly-for-profit
institution.

** Dragon Slayers' Academy reserves the right to keep some of the gold
and treasure that any student recovers from a dragon's lair.

*** The exact amount of treasure given to a student's family is determined
solely by our esteemed headmaster, Mordred. The amount shall be no less
than 1/500th of the treasure and no greater than 1/499th.

Mordred de Marvelous

Mordred graduated from Dragon Bludgeon High, second in his class. The other student, Lionel Flyzwattar, went on to become headmaster of Dragon Stabbers' Prep. Mordred spent years as part-time, semi-substitute student teacher at Dragon Whackers' Alternative School, all the while pursuing his passion for mud wrestling. Inspired by how filthy rich Flyzwattar had become by running a school, Mordred founded Dragon Slayers' Academy in CMLXXIV, and has served as headmaster ever since.

⚜

Known to the Boys as: Mordred de Miser
Dream: Piles and piles of dragon gold
Reality: Yet to see a single gold coin
Best-Kept Secret: Mud wrestled under the name Macho-Man Mordie
Plans for the Future: Will retire to the Bahamas . . . as soon as he gets his hands on a hoard

Lady Lobelia

Lobelia de Marvelous is Mordred's sister and a graduate of the exclusive If-You-Can-Read-This-You-Can-Design-Clothes Fashion School. Lobelia has offered fashion advice to the likes of King Felix the Husky and Eric the Terrible Dresser. In CMLXXIX, Lobelia married the oldest living knight, Sir Jeffrey Scabpicker III. That's when she gained the title of Lady Lobelia, but—alas!—only a very small fortune, which she wiped out in a single wild shopping spree. Lady Lobelia has graced Dragon Slayers' Academy with many visits, and can be heard around campus saying, "Just because I live in the Middle Ages doesn't mean I have to look middle-aged."

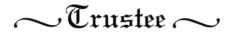

Known to the Boys as: Lady Lo Lo
Dream: Frightfully fashionable
Reality: Frightful
Best-Kept Secret: Shops at Dark-Age Discount Dress Dungeon
Plans for the Future: New uniforms for the boys with mesh tights and lace tunics

～Our Faculty～

Sir Mort du Mort

Sir Mort is our well-loved professor of Dragon Slaying. In his youth, he was known as the Scourge of Dragons. Sir Mort's last encounter was with the most dangerous dragon of them all: Knight-shredder. Early in the battle, Sir Mort took a nasty blow to his helmet and has never been the same since.

Coach Wendell Plungett

Coach Plungett spent many years questing in the Dark Forest before joining the Athletic Department. When he lef this dragon-slaying lays behind him, Coach Plungett was the manliest man to be found anywhere north of Nowhere Swamp. "I am what you call a hunk," the coach admits.

Brother Dave

Brother Dave is the DSA librarian. He belongs to the Little Brothers of the Peanut Brittle, an order known for doing impossibly good deeds and cooking up endless batches of peanut candy. After a batch of his extra-crunchy peanut brittle left three children toothless, Brother Dave vowed to do a truly impossible good deed. Thus did he offer to be librarian at a school world-famous for considering reading and writing a complete and utter waste of time.

Professor Prissius Pluck

Professor Pluck graduated from Peter Piper Picked a Peck of Pickled Peppers Prep, and went on to become a professor of science at Dragon Slayers' Academy. Boys who take Dragon Science, Professor Pluck's popular class, are amazed at the great quantities of saliva Professor P. can project and try never to sit in the front row.

Wiglaf of Pinwick

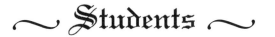

Wiglaf, our newest lad, hails from a hovel outside the village of Pinwick, which makes Toenail look like a thriving metropolis. Being one of thirteen children, Wiglaf had a taste of dorm life before coming to DSA and he fit right in. He started the year off with a bang when he took a stab at Coach Plungett's brown pageboy wig. Way to go, Wiggie! We hope to see more of this lad's wacky humor in the years to come.

❦

Dream: Bold Dragon-Slaying Hero
Reality: Still hangs on to a "security" rag
Extracurricular Activities: Animal-Lovers Club, President; No More Eel for Lunch Club, President; Frypot's Scrub Team, Brush Wielder; Pig Appreciation Club, Founder
Favorite Subject: Library
Oft-Heard Saying: *"Ello-hay, Aisy-day!"*
Plans for the Future: To go for the gold!

Eric von Royale

Eric hails from Someplace Far Away (at least that's what he wrote on his Application Form). There's an air of mystery about this Class I lad, who says he is "totally typical and absolutely average." If that is so, how did he come to own the rich tapestry that hangs over his cot? And are his parents really close personal friends of Sir Lancelot? Did Frypot the cook bribe him to start the Clean Plate Club? And doesn't Eric's arm ever get tired from raising his hand in class so often?

❦

Dream: Valiant Dragon Slayer
Reality: Teacher's Pet
Extracurricular Activities: Sir Lancelot Fan Club; Armor Polishing Club; Future Dragon Slayer of the Month Club; DSA Pep Squad, Founder and Cheer Composer
Favorite Subject: All of Them!!!!!
Oft-Heard Saying: *"When I am a mighty Dragon Slayer . . ."*
Plans for the Future: To take over DSA

Angus du Pangus

The nephew of Mordred and Lady Lobelia, Angus walks the line between saying, "I'm just one of the lads" and "I'm going to tell my uncle!" Will this Class I lad ever become a mighty dragon slayer? Or will he take over the kitchen from Frypot some day? We of the DSA Yearbook staff are betting on choice #2. And hey, Angus? The sooner the better!

⚜

Dream: A wider menu selection at DSA
Reality: Eel, Eel, Eel!
Extracurricular Activities: DSA Cooking Club, President; Smilin' Hal's Off-Campus Eatery, Sales Representative
Favorite Subject: Lunch
Oft-Heard Saying: *"I'm still hungry"*
Plans for the Future: To write *101 Ways to Cook a Dragon*

Baldrick de Bold

This is a banner year for Baldrick. He is celebrating his tenth year as a Class I lad at DSA. Way to go, Baldrick! If any of you new students want to know the ropes, Baldrick is the one to see. He can tell when you should definitely *not* eat the cafeteria's eel, where the choice seats are in Professor Pluck's class, and what to tell the headmaster if you are late to class. Just don't ask him the answer to any test questions.

❀

Dream: To run the world
Reality: A runny nose
Extracurricular Activities: Practice Dragon Maintenance Squad; Least Improved Slayer-in-Training Award
Favorite Subject: *"Could you repeat the question?"*
Oft Heard Saying: *"A dragon ate my homework."*
Plans for the Future: To transfer to Dragon Stabbers' Prep